Happy Ever After

Wedding Heat, Volume 15

Giselle Renarde

Published by Giselle Renarde, 2022.

First Edition August 2022

Happy Ever After

from the Wedding Heat series

Book 15

Giselle Renarde

"Beautiful place for a wedding," Betty said as she parked the car in Windhamwood Resort's overflow lot. "Remind me, dear: how are you related to the young bride?"

"I wouldn't call her a *young* bride," Margaret answered evasively. "I was nearly twenty-six when I married Charles, and Maggie is a darn sight older than that."

"Maggie?" Betty asked, snatching the wedding invite from Margaret's hand. "Is she named after you? You never did tell me who this girl is to you."

Margaret harrumphed. "Of course I told you. You must have forgotten."

"Well, then, tell me again."

"Where's the sense in that?" Margaret snipped. "Nothing sticks in your little brain."

Betty tittered. "Even so, I'd be keen on knowing whose wedding I'm about to attend."

Margaret's heart clenched. "The bride is of no relation. I sat for her mother when I was young—helped me pay for university. That's all there is to it."

"Oh," Betty replied.

Margaret tried not to flinch. She knew Betty could read her like a book.

Betty always seemed to know when she was lying, and said, "I thought a wealthy benefactor paid for your schooling."

"Nursing school, yes," Margaret replied. "During my first few years at university, I took on babysitting jobs in the neighbourhood. Tutoring, too. And each summer I worked at the—"

"Popsicle factory," Betty joined in. "Yes, I've heard that story so many times I could no doubt tell it myself. I just didn't know you'd ever babysat. I can't imagine you caring for children."

"Yes, well..." Margaret felt beads of sweat accumulating on her upper lip. She used the wedding invitation as a fan before saying, "Are we going to sit in this hot car all day, or shall we attend the ceremony?"

Betty checked her watch as Margaret pushed open the door. "We *are* a touch early, dear."

"I'd like to get my bearings," Margaret replied.

"Good idea. Very good. Perhaps a stroll around the grounds?"

Margaret had already walked away from the car by the time Betty emerged. The poor woman was breathing quite heavily by the time she caught up. "Would you look at that lake?" Betty said, pointing it out in the distance. "Isn't that a sight to behold!"

"Quite lovely," Margaret replied, watching the sun sparkle off its surface.

After a long moment looking out across the sprawling resort, Betty said, "I'm surprised you wanted to come. I thought you hated weddings."

Margaret felt quite puzzled by this revelation. "Who ever said I hated weddings?"

"You don't attend them very often."

"I'm not usually invited," Margaret reasoned.

"Strikes me as odd that you were invited to this one," Betty casually remarked as she brushed the wrinkles from her skirt. "You babysat the girl's mother, you say? Not exactly a close connection, is it?"

Taking the opportunity to change the subject, Margaret pointed across the sprawling expanse to where a huge white tent was set up. "That must be where the wedding will take place."

"Or the reception," Betty replied.

"They held the reception last night."

"Before the wedding?" Betty seemed scandalized. "I was hoping for a nip."

"I'm afraid you're plum out of luck. They're putting out high tea after the ceremony, but no alcohol. That way nobody drives home intoxicated."

"Well, yes, I suppose that's perfectly reasonable," Betty said as she bumbled down the hillock toward the lake. "I was just in the mood for a tipple, that's all."

Betty's turn of phrase sent Margaret barreling back to the distant past, to the time in her life that had landed her at this very wedding. Every sense ignited as she remembered sitting in the Bensons' front room with her purse in her lap, finished for the evening and waiting only for her wages. The children were long in bed and she'd spent much of the night at her studies.

"Can I offer you a tipple before you take off?" Dr. Benson had asked.

The offer surprised her, because it implied that the doctor saw her as an equal. For a man who was not only a medical practitioner but also as handsome as Rock Hudson to offer Margaret a drink was truly unprecedented in her life.

Before she could say no thank you, that she really ought to be getting home, Dr. Benson's darling wife clucked, "Oh, Fred! You shouldn't be offering the girl alcohol. She isn't yet twenty-one!"

"I'm afraid I am, Mrs. Benson," Margaret interrupted. "I turned twenty-one not three weeks ago."

The lady of the house seemed distracted by the task of removing her evening gloves. She barely took the time to remark, "Silly me—I thought you were the student."

"Yes, that's right," Margaret continued. "I'm a university student, Mrs. Benson, not a high school girl."

"You're thinking of that other sitter we had," Dr. Benson cut in. "Tricia was her name."

"Oh, yes, that's right." Mrs. Benson turned as though she had only just realized Margaret existed. "And you are...?"

"I'm Margaret, Mrs. Benson. Margaret Miller."

"Oh, that's right—Margaret. It's all coming back to me now. You're the one who's going through to be a nurse."

"That's always been my aspiration, Mrs. Benson."

Looking Margaret up and down, Mrs. Benson remarked, "Wise choice. Plain girls do well in careers, don't you think so, Fred?" Turning her icy gaze on her husband, she went on to say, "That other girl, Trixie—"

"Tricia."

"Yes, Tricia. She was a pretty young thing. I believe she's married now."

"That's right," her husband replied. He offered an apologetic chuckle, and then said, "We lose more babysitters that way."

"Quite," Mrs. Benson chirped as she swept off into the hallway.

"You'll pardon my wife," Dr. Benson said quietly. "She's terribly forgetful when it comes to names."

"Of course," Margaret replied, with the understanding that he was apologizing for so much more. He was clearly embarrassed by his wife's remarks, though they were nothing Margaret hadn't heard from teachers and aunts.

"You'll have a drink, then?" the doctor asked.

From another room, Mrs. Benson clucked, "Goodness, Fred, would you pay Trixie for the evening and let her go? A girl in her teens wants to get out with friends, not sit around with an old fuddy-duddy like you."

"Actually, I'm not in my teens," Margaret uttered, though the lady of the house had already swept up the stairs by the time she'd opened her mouth. "And my name isn't Trixie."

When Margaret met Dr. Benson's kindly gaze, he tilted his head knowingly. "My wife..."

"No need," Margaret cut in. She always found it awkward when men made apologies for the women in their lives. It was hardly the doctor's fault that he'd married a bubble-brained little madame. "I ought to be on my way, at any rate."

When Margaret rose from her seat, so did the doctor. He asked, "Can I drive you home, Miss Miller?"

"Thank you, no," she replied. "I live very close-by: only a hop, skip and a jump away."

The turn of phrase made her feel silly and childish, and she didn't know why she'd put it that way.

Dr. Benson smiled congenially. He went to the mantel and plucked from it an envelope. Clearly, this was her pay for the evening. She traced her fingers across own name, Margaret Miller, admiring the script. "Your wife has fine handwriting, Dr. Benson."

He burbled and blushed before admitting, "It's actually my handwriting, that."

A flush came over her. She bowed her head to hide while tucking the envelope neatly into her purse.

"I know what you're thinking," the doctor went on.

On alert, Margaret asked, “Do you?”

“Why, certainly.”

Margaret gulped, feeling horribly flustered.

“You thought all doctors had chicken-scratch handwriting, didn't you?” He chuckled to himself. “Patients comment all the time.”

A wave of relief came over Margaret and she went along with the doctor's version. “Yes, quite.”

What she had, in fact, been thinking was that she'd never come across a man who took care of household tasks, such as organizing the babysitter's pay packet. It seemed more than a little unusual that Mrs. Benson hadn't written out the envelope herself.

What did the woman do all day?

“Thank you, again,” Margaret said to the doctor as she made her way toward the door.

“I should be thanking you,” he replied. “Let me show you out.”

The doctor followed at a respectable distance, and opened the door as she bent to lace her saddle shoes.

Before leaving, Margaret said, “I hope you don't find me too forward in saying this, but...”

His eyes widened, and she struggled for breath.

“...but if you should find yourself in need of a babysitter in the near future, I hope you'll consider me first. The children and I got on smashingly, and I was able to help them with their schoolwork after dinner. They went to bed without a fuss after I read to them. It was a perfectly successful evening.”

“Glad to hear it.” Dr. Benson patted Margaret gently on the shoulder. “I assure you we'll be in touch.”

"IF ONLY WE'D BROUGHT a bag of bread," Betty blustered as they looked across the small lake.

Shaking away her tender memories, Margaret asked, "Bread? What ever do we need with bread?"

Betty indicated the waterfowl swimming along the shoreline. "We could feed the ducks."

"Those are geese," Margaret replied. "And, anyway, you're not supposed to feed them bread."

"Why not?"

In a haughty tone, Margaret said, "Bread makes their stomachs explode."

"We used to feed the ducks all the time when I was young. I never saw any stomachs explode."

"Well, you wouldn't, would you? It's not as if you're shoving them full of TNT. The effect isn't quite so dramatic as that." In hopes of shifting the topic once more, Margaret said, "Let's see if we can't find a washroom before heading to the tent."

"Good idea," Betty said. "This sunshine is doing my head in."

"You ought to have worn a hat with a wider brim," Margaret told her.

"Right you are, right you are! Remind me next time. You know how I forget."

DR. BENSON STOOD AT Margaret's side as they watched the children frolic in the shallows. After a time, he said, "This was a wonderful idea, spending a day at the beach. I'm so glad you thought of it."

"I can't take all the credit," Margaret confessed. "All week, the children have been moaning about missing their mother. I figured, since she's spending the summer at the lake house, coming to the waterfront might help them feel a touch closer to her."

"A splendid idea," the doctor replied. "In two weeks' time, the children will join Norma by the lake and you'll be free to take up your shifts at the popsicle factory. I'll bet the factory pays a darn sight better than sitting for three rugrats and a frazzled old doctor."

"Old? Far from it," Margaret said, instantly regretting the utterance. She switched tracks quite deliberately, telling him, "I shall miss seeing the children every day."

"I dare say they'll miss you as well," the doctor replied, wrapping a carefree arm around her shoulder.

Margaret had never been so close to a man. She'd been on dates with boys from school, and yes there had been a certain amount of necking involved, but she didn't consider that crowd to be in the same league as a debonaire gentleman like Dr. Benson. Now he was close enough beside her that she could smell his pipe tobacco and the medicinal odour of his professional practice, as well as the lingering aroma of aftershave he'd surely slapped on more than eight hours prior.

Generally, Margaret wore a simple skirt suit for her days of sitting the doctor's children. Because they had planned this beach day, she'd worn clamdiggers and a loose-fitting blouse. Although many young women at the beach were showing far more than bare ankles, Margaret felt rather brazen in her chosen ensemble.

As for the doctor, he had removed his shoes and socks the minute he arrived to collect Margaret and the children. Not only that, but he'd rolled up his pant legs halfway to the knees in order not to get his trousers wet while he paddled in the shallows.

He was quite the devoted father, Dr. Benson was. Margaret had never met another man quite like him.

And there he stood beside her, so close her hip faintly brushed his, while he cast a forgetful arm around her shoulder. The manner in which he leaned his weight on her ever so slightly made her feel as though she were holding him upright while his wife was away.

Margaret had never felt so proud. She hoped someone she knew might see her standing this way with the handsome doctor. Perhaps the teachers she'd known from school, the ones who'd advised her to take up a career because only the pretty girls could count on finding husbands, would think twice about what they'd said after viewing her in what might be mistaken for a type of embrace.

"You'll join us for dinner, I hope," Dr. Benson said, giving Margaret's shoulder a jaunty squeeze before reaching for his socks.

Margaret bashfully turned away while the doctor shook sand from his shoes. "Only if you'll allow me to help you prepare it this time."

"True, last night was a bit of a disaster," he replied with a laugh.

Margaret felt her face turning red, and not just from the sun. "That isn't at all what I meant, Dr. Benson! Please forgive me if my comment sounded unflattering. I only meant that it wouldn't be fair to you, after working all day long, to come home and prepare a meal all on your own."

"You've been working the whole day, too," the doctor reasoned. "You've been taking care of my children. And a fine job you've done of it."

Her face reddened all the more. "I dare say, the little imps will sleep tonight."

"I dare say so will you!" the doctor replied.

Margaret wasn't so certain. She'd endured more than a few sleepless nights since Mrs. Benson left for the lake house.

"HAVE YOU EVER SEEN so many guests at a wedding?" Betty gasped, placing her hand across her heart.

Margaret murmured her response as she searched for faces she might recognize. After so many years, how could she hope to identify the children she'd cared for? How would they recognize her?

Did she want to be recognized, or would she prefer to remain anonymous?

Ought she introduce herself to the bride?

And to the mother of the bride?

After so many years of separation, would she recognize her own child?

"Look here," Betty called out. "I suppose those trailers have washrooms inside."

Now that they found themselves in and among the crowd, Margaret had trouble tearing her attention away.

"Would you look at that queue," Betty went on. "We had better get in line or we're likely to miss the ceremony!"

"I'm not so keen on using a washroom in a trailer," Margaret grumbled.

A woman passing by overheard her comment and said, "The washrooms are great! Cost an arm and a leg to rent, according to my sister-in-law, so don't be shy!"

Her sister-in-law? That wouldn't be the mother of the bride, by any chance?

Margaret missed her opportunity to ask. The woman was already lost in the crowd.

And even if she got the chance to meet the daughter she'd given up all those years ago, would she take advantage? Today of all days, when the girl—when the *woman*—would be caught up in the drama of her own daughter's wedding?

No, today was not the time to impose herself on the daughter she'd never met. If she'd been able to work up the nerve, she'd have come forward when her daughter sent her the invitation to this event, along with a handwritten note saying, "I would love to finally meet you."

Margaret had been less distressed upon receiving this wedding invitation than she'd been when Sharon had first reached out. "It would be nice to get to know you," her daughter had written. "Everything can be on your terms. We could exchange letters or talk on the phone or even meet in person if you're up for that. Whatever makes you most comfortable."

The letter had brought angry tears to Margaret's eyes. How dare this girl be so caring and compassionate after Margaret had callously walked away from her? Sharon ought to hate the woman who bore her. She ought to hate Margaret as much as Margaret hated herself.

"My father explained everything after my mother died," Sharon had gone on in her letter. "I want you to know that I don't hold your choices against you. I don't judge you in any way. You were young when you got pregnant with me. You had your whole life ahead of you. You did what you needed to do. I respect you and I love you. I want you to hold that truth inside your heart."

Margaret never told a soul she'd received such a letter. She hadn't even confessed the facts of her premarital life to Charles. As far as her late husband knew, she came to their marriage bed a virgin.

How far was that from the truth?

WITH THE WEEKEND OFF from her job at the factory, Margaret made her way to the Benson house. She knew the children would be at the lake with their mother by now. If the doctor happened to be outside, what then? Why, she'd say hello, naturally. If he asked what brought her 'round, she would say she'd opted for a stroll before the weather got too warm.

And if he asked her why she'd worn her best summer skirt suit and gloves simply to stroll around the neighbourhood, how would she respond?

It wouldn't come to that. Dr. Benson would never ask something so uncouth.

When she arrived a short distance from the house, her heart stopped. There was Dr. Benson! Out front, just as she'd hoped! He was attired casually, in woollen trousers and without a jacket. His shirtsleeves were neatly folded up. He wore a heavy pair of leather gloves as he pruned the overgrown roses that had taken off around the arbour.

"Dr. Benson!" Margaret called from the sidewalk. "Lovely morning to work in the garden."

The doctor turned abruptly. A smile broke across his lips when he realized who had called to him. "Miss Miller!" he replied. "Lovely morning indeed."

Margaret prepared herself to answer any question he might put forth, but rather than asking what brought her to the house, he simply said, "Norma generally handles the garden—she's got the green thumb in our household—but seeing as she's out of town for the time being, I thought it judicious to cut back some of these roses."

"They'll look dandy in a vase," Margaret agreed, eying the cream-coloured blossoms.

"I ought to send you home with a few buds," he offered. "Brighten up the student lodgings."

"You're too kind," Margaret replied, blushing wildly as he went indoors to fetch newsprint to wrap the stems so she wouldn't be pricked by thorns. How many men were so considerate as Dr. Benson? Oh, and wouldn't the other girls be jealous when she brought home roses from an admirer? The best they received from their beaus were carnations and daisies.

Margaret beamed as the doctor wrapped a large bouquet of roses in yesterday's news. "You are too kind," she told him. "And ever so thoughtful."

As he handed the bouquet to her over the whitewashed pickets, he said, "I'm loath to cut our conversation short, but I really must wash up. I've offered to check in on a patient at ten."

"Oh, I see," Margaret replied, feeling let down in the extreme.

How silly of her, to think that a man like Dr. Benson would care to wile away his time with the likes of Miss Margaret Miller. She was nowhere near as glamorous as his own wife, and her looks paled vastly in comparison.

"Thank you for the roses," she began as she stepped away from his sprawling property. "I do hope you'll find time in your day for enjoyment. It is the weekend, after all."

"All work and no play makes Jack a dull boy," the doctor answered back.

Margaret nodded cheerlessly.

She had already turned to take her leave when the doctor spoke. "Miss Miller?"

Thinking she had perhaps dropped something, Margaret glanced back at Dr. Benson.

He went on to say, "With Norma away, I haven't enjoyed a good meal in some time. I'm not the world's greatest chef, as you can attest."

"You mustn't cook everything at such a high heat," Margaret reminded him. "That's why your meat burns on the outside when it's not yet cooked on the inside." Finding an undeniable boldness inside herself, she proposed, "I could come over this evening to teach you how it's done. I'm an excellent cook, myself. And it's really very simple once you know what you're doing."

Taking a few steps closer to the picket fence, the doctor said, "I appreciate the offer, Miss Miller, but what would the neighbours say if they spotted a handsome young woman entering a married man's home while his wife was known to be summering by the lake?"

A shameful flush consumed Margaret's face. With tears in her eyes, she apologized to the doctor for putting him in such an uncomfortable predicament.

"You've done nothing of the sort," he assured her. "In point of fact, I was about to say that I've never been fond of dining alone."

"I can certainly relate," Margaret agreed, sniffling as she dug into her purse in search of a handkerchief.

"After so much rotten cooking," the doctor went on, "I'd say I'm in desperate need of a steak prepared by expert hands. What say I pick you up this evening around seven and treat the two of us to a fine meal? There's a little place in town that I really don't get to often enough."

Margaret couldn't believe these words were truly coming out of the doctor's mouth. Could she possibly be misinterpreting his intention, or was he asking her out for the evening?

In fear that he might change his mind, or suddenly come to his senses, Margaret said, "I would love to have dinner with you, Dr. Benson. You know where I live?"

"I do indeed, Miss Miller."

What luck! What perfectly astronomical luck! The girls she lodged with wouldn't believe it. No, she mustn't let on. Not just yet. Just in case she'd made some sort of mistake. Perhaps she was misinterpreting kindness or loneliness as romantic intention.

She wouldn't tell anybody she was going to dinner with the doctor this evening.

Margaret walked on air all the way home. Even when she noticed that her white gloves had turned grey from the newsprint wrapped around her roses, she could not be dissuaded from believing that her blossoming romance with Dr. Benson would surely work out well.

AFTER TWO HOURS IN the car with Betty, Margaret was eager to get away from the old girl. They'd been friends for decades, but she found Betty's voice grating. And the constant chatter, goodness gracious! One couldn't find a moment's peace with Betty around.

There was still plenty of time before the ceremony, and everything was late starting nowadays. There wasn't the same respect for time that existed in years gone by.

Margaret made her way toward the hotel and lied to the receptionist in order to gain entry. Apparently wedding guests were indeed meant to use the facilities in those trailers outdoors, but Margaret made her way to the WC by the hotel lounge. The moment alone was akin to bliss after the chaos she'd encountered outdoors. Betty was right about one thing: she had never seen so many guests at a wedding, or at any other gathering, from what she could recall.

After she'd relieved herself in pure and glorious silence, Margaret parked her keister at a window seat in the lounge. When an attractive young waiter came by, she surprised herself by ordering an old-fashioned. While she waited for her drink to arrive, she gazed out the window, searching the milling throngs for the family she'd never known.

"Here you are," the waiter said, placing her drink on a small napkin. "One old-fashioned. Is there anything else I can get for you?"

"Thank you, no. This drink looks wonderful."

With loving appreciation, Margaret admired the way the orange peel hugged the large cube of ice in her glass. As she lifted it to her lips and prepared herself for the bittersweet sting of alcohol, she was transported back to the night she'd first tasted this drink. It was a night of many firsts, for Margaret.

Dr. Benson picked her up from her student lodgings at seven on the dot, as they'd arranged. Because it was so rare for her to go out in the evening, the girls with whom she shared her abode insisted on fussing over her: applying a heavy layer of cosmetics and backcombing her hair, selecting which outfit she ought to wear. In fact, the girls settled on clothes from one another's closets, as it was commonly agreed that Margaret's own apparel wouldn't do for a Saturday night.

"Who is this mystery man?" they kept asking, but she wouldn't tell. She could only hope they wouldn't recognize the doctor's aging Merc when it pulled up out front.

Though she knew it defied all known etiquette, she raced out the door the moment he arrived.

The frock her girlfriends had selected for her was a high-cut satin number overlaid with a drape of lace and cinched above the waistline with a smart-looking ribbon. The satin and lace were in matching shades of a blue so deep it was almost black, while the ribbon gleamed startling white. She hoped to keep it that way. The last thing she wanted was to order something saucy that might stain a white ribbon red. Goodness knows how many shifts she'd have to work at the factory in order to pay her housemate back for such a terrible faux pas.

Margaret didn't give the doctor time to step out of his car, much less circle it and open her door for her. She popped open the passenger side and slipped into her seat before he could reach for the latch.

"I apologize," Margaret bleated. "I don't intend to seem too eager, only I know the girls are watching out the front window and... well..."

"Say no more," the doctor replied. "I must tell you, Miss Miller, I've never seen you looking so elegant."

"Thank you." She felt glad he was driving so he wouldn't notice her terrible blush. "I had a lot of help from the girls at home. It wasn't my intention to appear so glamorous."

"You'll fit right in where we're headed," Dr. Benson told her.

Her stomach knotted when they pulled up outside a posh hotel in town.

Margaret gaped as she entered on the doctor's arm. "This is where we're eating?"

"Unless you'd rather dine elsewhere."

The doctor stepped toward the maitre d' and said he had a reservation, but he gave the name of Ben Smith rather than his own. Margaret flushed upon hearing this. The only people who gave false names at restaurants were film stars and men cheating on their wives.

To the best of Margaret's knowledge, Dr. Benson was not a film star.

A rush of terror consumed Margaret's stomach as the maitre d' escorted them to an isolated table. The doctor pulled out her chair and she sat warily. As he pressed her chair in, he set a warm hand on her shoulder. The frightened feeling washed away. His touch was all she needed to feel warmth and comfort. His patients must adore him for his bedside manner.

Perhaps Margaret would find out tonight.

No! What a thought to have. And Dr. Benson a married man. A married man with three young children. Three young children who had recently been in Margaret's charge.

These thoughts of hers were evil, evil indeed. And yet, if these thoughts were evil, she hoped never again to have good ones.

Evil intension twisted like a snake in her belly.

Whatever the doctor desired, she would surely do.

He ordered her a steak, same as he was having, and a Chateau Petrus she barely sipped at.

"Is your steak too rare?" he asked when she only picked at her food. "I can call the waiter."

"No, no," she assured the doctor. "It's fine. Only, this dress belongs to one of the other girls and it is a little tight around the middle."

"Well, isn't that a shame?" he replied, forking a tender square of meat into his mouth and chewing with delight. "It's been a long, long while since I've had a meal of this quality."

Margaret worried that she was wasting the doctor's money by not consuming the food he'd ordered for her, and she made a renewed effort to eat. She came nowhere near finishing every bite on her plate. When the waiter asked if she was done, she nodded demurely.

The doctor looked at her across the table and asked, "Dessert?"

"Oh, I couldn't possibly, Dr. Ben—" She remembered halfway through saying his name that he'd provided a false one to the restaurant, and so she halted.

"You'll have an aperitif, though, surely," the doctor said before ordering them each an old-fashioned.

As they awaited their drinks, Margaret folded her hands politely in her lap, though the doctor appeared to be reaching for her across the empty table. To her left, a small candle burnt in a solid red holder. The light it cast upon the white tablecloth flickered unsteadily as she ventured one hand out of her lap and across the expanse.

Before the doctor's fingers could find hers, the waiter returned with their aperitifs.

"Ah!" said the doctor, rubbing his palms together eagerly. "Our drinks have arrived!"

Margaret's pulse raced when she caught sight of the twist of orange rind resting across the top of her glass. She followed the doctor's lead of dropping it onto the drink before taking a sip. She hadn't expected it to taste sweet, but she was glad that it did. The alcohol grasped her throat unexpected, causing her to cough, which she found terribly embarrassing in front of the debonair doctor.

He smiled gently and said, "Take smaller sips, perhaps."

She took his advice, but the alcohol still burned. Less so with every sip, though. When she discovered the lovely nuance of the orange peel, she found she appreciated its ability to convey brightness and bitterness simultaneously.

As Margaret sipped her old-fashioned in the empty lounge at Windhamwood Resort, she reflected upon the nature of memory: focus could be turned on the brightness or the bitterness, just as with this drink. It was only a matter of perspective.

While Margaret considered that it might be time to settle her bill, a young woman in bridal apparel stormed into the lounge. Hot on her heels was a lovely young lady—one of the bridesmaids, judging by her ghastly gown—saying, "Maggie! Maggie, come back here!"

"No!" said the bride. "I'm not a dog."

"I know you're not a dog."

"Then stop treating me like one!"

The bride marched to the corner of the lounge. She folded her arms petulantly across her large chest and stared out the window at the very scene Margaret had been observing. All those people out there had come here to celebrate the girl's love. Margaret had merely come to celebrate the girl.

"Nobody's treating you like a dog," the bridesmaid went on, though she was clearly overwhelmed with frustration as she said those words. "We just want to keep tabs on you today, that's all."

Swivelling gently, Maggie asked, "Why? Why can't I have a moment to myself?"

Her bridesmaid came close enough to place both hands on Maggie's bare shoulders. "Because you're a flight risk and you're supposed to get married twenty minutes from now."

A conspiratorial smile bled across the bride's pretty lips. The girls considered each other wordlessly, communicating in a way only close friends could. A strain of envy passed through Margaret's system as she observed them together. Had she ever in her life enjoyed a friendship as close as theirs? Had she ever truly shared her thoughts with anybody?

Her husband, perhaps, but even he never knew the full truth.

As the bride and bridesmaid embraced cautiously—careful not to damage their gowns, hair or makeup—Margaret looked on as though she were watching a film. She found it nearly impossible to believe that this young woman was her granddaughter, although she knew it to be true. She'd thought she might find certain feelings inside herself, when she saw the girl for the first time, but that was not Margaret's experience. She felt about the bride the way she might feel around any bride on the day of her wedding: hopeful and cautious and filled to the brim with baseless nostalgia.

"Oh, Pippa," Maggie muttered, hugging her bridesmaid a little tighter. "What if he doesn't show up?"

Pippa laughed. "He's probably saying the same thing about you."

Stomping her heel on the ground, Maggie erupted with an unprecedented spew of anger. "This isn't cold feet! I'm worried he won't show because he *said* he wouldn't show. Not twenty-four hours ago, Ed said he wouldn't marry me. He broke it off and walked away from me forever."

"Yeah, but he didn't stay away," Pippa encouraged her, toying with the bride's honey-coloured curls. "The two of you talked it out this morning. He forgives you, Maggs. You know in your heart that's true."

"It was true when he said it," Maggie reasoned. "What if he changed his mind? What if someone talked him out of marrying me? Or what if he talked himself out of it?"

"Or what if a tornado swept by and plucked him off the face of the earth?" Pippa teased. "You can 'what if' yourself to death if you really want to, but what would be the point? You've got a wedding ceremony scheduled in twenty—make that fifteen—minutes. You know that man's gonna show, I know that man's gonna show, he knows perfectly well he's gonna show, so what is there to be afraid of? Let's do this thing, Maggie. Let's do it."

Pippa's impassioned speech very nearly gave Margaret the guts to introduce herself as the bride's long-lost grandmother, but just as she rose from her seat, she heard a voice from the lounge entrance: "Maggie, honey, there you are! We've been looking all over the place."

"Sorry, Mom," the bride replied. "Everything's fine. Here I am."

Feeling as though she were in a dream, Margaret turned to catch sight of the woman her granddaughter had called "Mom."

Her name was Sharon. That was the name Margaret had given her at birth, and that was the name she had kept all her life, according to her brief correspondence.

Yes, the full-figured woman in the cream-coloured mother-of-the-bride's outfit was undoubtedly Margaret's daughter, and yet, upon seeing her, Margaret felt no connection—only a morbid fascination. This morbid fascination was, however, coupled with a brand of numbness that caused her heart to become a block of ice inside her chest.

The woman at the lounge entrance bore no resemblance to the baby Margaret had birthed, though why should she? How many adults grew up looking like their babyhood selves?

Two more bridesmaids flanked the mother-of-the-bride, and one of these young women said, "Get your ass in gear!"

Sharon tittered nervously, probably feeling as uncomfortable with the uncouth girl's cursing as Margaret felt. Perhaps these things run in the family.

"Yes, come along, Maggie," Sharon said to her daughter. "If we leave Ed alone at the altar too long, he might start thinking you've had a change of heart."

Pippa and Maggie exchanged collusive glances before the bride took off across the lounge. She leapt at her mother as a child would do, and they hugged one another with a kind of shameless familial glee Margaret had never known.

Margaret had to admit she felt dazed as she watched this sparkling show of affection. Her own mother had worn a stern scowl on her wedding day, knowing what she knew.

After a lengthy and affectionate maternal embrace, Sharon glanced at her watch. "We really should get going now, Maggie. Mustn't keep a man waiting much longer than it takes to fix your lipstick."

Maggie laughed with her mother as they left the lounge. "Is that another one of your wifely pearls of wisdom?"

The bridesmaids laughed along, spouting such gems as, "Don't cook the same meal two nights in a row," and, "Mix him a drink when he walks through the door!"

Margaret stood on shaky legs to watch them walk away. Her daughter and her granddaughter. They hadn't even noticed her sitting there, watching their exchange. Perhaps the psychic bonds one hears about in books and films are the stuff of fiction. Margaret saw no evidence of it in Sharon and Maggie, nor did she sense it in her bones.

Every moment since her arrival at Windhamwood Resort had felt surreal, as if she were visiting an alternate universe.

Slipping far too much cash from her purse, she left the young waiter a hefty tip and followed the gaggle of giggling bridesmaids out of the lounge. She could see the whole group of them leaving the resort building by a doorway at the end of the hall, but she couldn't bring herself to follow. She couldn't say whether it was the drink or the experience of seeing her daughter and granddaughter for the first time, but Margaret needed the toilet.

Immediately.

MARGARET KNEW SHE WAS spending far too much time in the restroom. The doctor wouldn't wait forever. She couldn't seem to open the door, much less reach for the doorknob, much less turn her attention away from her reflection in the mirror.

The girl she saw before her was not the real Margaret. The real Margaret was plain of face. She wore her hair in a simply ponytail. Strawberry was not her usual shade of lipstick, and yet she couldn't bring herself to wipe it away. She didn't have a more subdued hue in her date purse.

If the doctor wanted a glamour girl, why not stick with his wife? Norma was by far the most glamorous woman Margaret had ever met. He must prefer his women looking this way.

And yet, if that were true, why step out with Margaret?

Margaret's thoughts spun out of control until a knock at the door brought the world into sharp focus.

"Miss Miller?" the doctor asked gently. "Is everything all right in there? I don't mean to disturb you, only—"

"I'm sorry!" Margaret bleated. "I've been ever so long reapplying my lipstick." She didn't want the doctor thinking she was doing anything else. "I'm coming out now."

Still, she couldn't tear her gaze away from her own reflection. She looked desperately pale, despite the thick coating of foundation her housemates had applied. Her lashes fluttered as she begged herself not to cry. What was there to cry about?

Margaret unlocked the bathroom door and stepped into the hotel room Dr. Benson had secured for them. She'd watched over his shoulder as he signed them in as Mr. and Mrs. Ben Smith.

False names. Fraudulent identities. She felt like a criminal.

Never in her life has she done anything so daring.

The moment Margaret opened the door, Dr. Benson held out her wrap. "Perhaps I ought to take you home, Miss Miller."

Margaret glanced at her watch. They'd entered this hotel room half an hour ago. Had she really spent half an hour staring at herself in the bathroom mirror? She felt stupefied. "But why would we leave? We've only just arrived."

The doctor set a gentle hand on her shoulder and said, "I think perhaps it was wrong-headed of me to check us into this room, Miss Miller. I've enjoyed our evening tremendously. I wouldn't want to ruin the memory by pushing you prematurely into an encounter for which you're unprepared."

She wanted to shout out, "I am prepared!" but on what basis? The thought of going to bed with the doctor, or with any man, caused her face to flush and her insides to knot. It was true: she did not feel prepared for love in any sense.

Surely she would know when the time was right.

Surely she would have some sense of deep resonance with the man.

But did she not share such a connection with the doctor? She thought she did. Now she wasn't sure. If their connection were as intense as all that, would they not fall into bed as naturally as could be? Would passion not overtake them? Would he not sweep her into his arms and kiss her with force and press her onto the pillows?

"Come, Miss Miller," the doctor said as he escorted her to the door. "Let me take you home."

Margaret didn't wish to kick up a fuss, and so she walked with him in tension-filled silence. As he drove her home, he made a valiant attempt to elicit any form of conversation from her. When he proved unsuccessful in his attempt, he asked if she would like to turn on the radio.

She softly whimpered, "Thank you, no," and they rode along without music.

The house was dark when Margaret arrived home. No surprises, there. It was Saturday night, after all. The girls had gone out.

Dr. Benson walked her to the door and thanked her for a lovely evening. She said nothing, only stared up at him in hopes of a kiss.

He planted a chaste peck on her cheek and bid her goodnight.

As he began to walk away, she blurted, "Would you like to come inside, Dr. Benson?"

He seemed stunned by the suggestion, and glanced over his shoulder, at the houses across the street. "I think not, Miss Miller. Perhaps a friendly visit, someday, when your housemates are at home."

"Yes, of course," she said. "You're welcome any time."

She watched him walk to his car and waved. At first, when he failed to leave, she thought perhaps he might change his mind and come in for a drink. They didn't keep alcohol in the house, but she could certainly offer him coffee, tea, or cocoa.

After a long moment of staring at the Mercury, Margaret realized why he hadn't yet departed: he was waiting for her to get in the house safely. This realization stole the wind from her sails, and she slowly turned to enter.

Once inside, she raced to the front window and watched forlornly while the doctor drove away.

Though Margaret had been home alone on many a Saturday night, the house had never felt so stiflingly still. She kicked off her shoes and paced the front room until her nylons caught on the floorboards. She told herself to stop being silly and maudlin, to head upstairs, put on her nightdress, and get into bed.

The bed at the hotel had been remarkably modern. She hadn't given herself a chance to take in her surroundings at the time, but thinking back, she realized how sleek the furnishings had been. Clean lines, walnut or teak—she wasn't sure which.

Everything Margaret owned was inherited from family members. Not a contemporary piece in sight. She wondered if the doctor liked that style better, or if he—like Margaret herself—preferred older items.

All at once, she felt a burning desire to know how Dr. Benson felt about contemporary home furnishings. Did he love the new style? Did he detest it? Margaret couldn't live another day without knowing.

Slipping on her everyday walking shoes—and not the heels her girlfriend had leant her—Margaret grabbed the light wrap Dr. Benson had handed her when she'd exited the hotel bathroom. She cringed when she thought about that moment. He had rejected her, well and truly. Why? She couldn't say.

Perhaps she'd taken so long in the WC that he'd decided she mustn't want to be there with him. Perhaps he believed she was hiding. Perhaps she *had* been hiding, in some small sense. But not from the doctor! Hiding from her own fear of desire. The act they intended to engage in was considered sinful by many. It was a decision not to be taken lightly.

Despite her many fears and self-recriminations, Margaret opened the front door and let herself loose on the night.

BETTY STOOD ALONE OUTSIDE the large white wedding tent as Margaret approached it.

"Where have you been?" Betty scolded her. "I've said it once and I'll say it again: you will be the death of me, woman!"

When Margaret peeked inside the tent, she saw tables set up but nobody sitting in the elegantly-appointed chairs.

Flush with alarm, Margaret asked Betty, "What happened? Did the groom call it off?"

Giving Margaret an odd look, Betty said, "Nobody called anything off. The ceremony's taking place on the dock. Don't you see? It's about to begin. Let's shake a leg!"

Margaret had never seen her friend move so quickly in all the years of their acquaintance. Clearly, Betty didn't want to miss the wedding.

And there was Margaret, thinking the old girl had only come along for the free food.

When Margaret turned to follow her friend, she wondered how on earth she'd managed to miss the masses of guests seated by the lake. They made their way down a paved path lined with lovely blooms.

Soon enough, Margaret realized there was a string quartet playing something familiar—Vivaldi, perhaps. If she were in a less frazzled state of mind, she could say for certain. As it stood,

Margaret felt utterly panicked. She might miss the very ceremony they'd driven all this way to see.

"Hurry up!" Betty huffed as she trotted down the path's slight incline. "We're going to miss the moment when they say *I do*!"

"Don't get your knickers in a twist," Margaret said. "The ceremony hasn't started yet. Look ahead, there. It's only the minister and the groom standing out on that dock. The bride is nowhere in sight."

"Use your eyes!" Betty cried, indicating a grouping of women in gowns. "The bride's right there."

The sight of her granddaughter stopped Margaret in her tracks. Betty clearly didn't notice that she'd come to a halt, because the old girl kept on down the hill while Margaret stood agog. She couldn't even say why she reacted this way. Only moments ago, she'd observed an entire conversation between the bride and her bridesmaid, and then between the bride and her mother.

But that experience in the hotel lounge had felt like a dream.

Margaret felt the shocking sting of reality as she stared across the expanse. This was no daydream, no fantasy or illusion. That beaming young woman in the gracious white gown was her granddaughter. The woman smiling softly as Maggie prepared to walk down the aisle was Margaret's own daughter.

How could she possibly attend this wedding?

And yet, how could she turn her back on it?

Betty arrived at the last row of seats just as the string quartet struck up a lovely rendition of another familiar tune Margaret couldn't put her finger on. The old girl must have thought

Margaret was just behind her, because she seemed perplexed when she turned to find herself alone.

The flower girl started down the centre aisle leading up to the dock.

Betty waved in a panic, mouthing, "The ceremony is starting!"

Margaret must get a move on.

WHEN MARGARET ARRIVED at the doctor's house, she entered by the kitchen door. The front door would most likely have been left unlocked as well, but she'd have felt suspicious entering his residence at this hour in plain sight of the neighbours.

She snuck in the back way, under cover of darkness.

The house was dead quiet, and she wondered, for a moment, if the doctor was even home. Perhaps he hadn't returned after dropping her off. Perhaps he'd gone to seek comfort from some other girl in his acquaintance.

That's when she noticed the sliver of second-storey light illuminating the staircase from above. She then heard a squeak, which sounded like bedsprings. Had the doctor come home and immediately readied himself for bed?

Or was he up there with someone else?

Had Norma come home from the lake house?

No, certainly not. If Mrs. Benson were at home, the house would be overwhelmed by her endless chatter.

Margaret shrugged off her jacket and placed it lightly on the back of a chair. She also removed her shoes so their click-clacking sounds would not alert the doctor to her presence in his home.

Had she come to surprise him in bed? This hadn't been her initial plan, but if the doctor was indeed in bed—and if he was alone—she would indeed take him by surprise.

And if he wasn't alone?

He would no doubt be surprised regardless.

Margaret was very familiar with the house. She'd spent enough time there, caring for the children. She knew which stairs creaked, and took pains to avoid them. Her heart pounded in her ears as she made her way to the second floor. She grasped the bannister firmly, feeling as though a waterfall of resistance were pushing against her.

She tried with all her might to turn off the part of her brain that wouldn't stop nagging. *She ought not be here. A good girl wouldn't. He's married. He has three children.*

And yet she could not bear for him to think of her as a tease. She had wants and desires like any other girl. Just because she hadn't expressed them yet didn't mean they were not there.

The door to the doctor's bedroom was open. When Margaret arrived at the top of the stairs, she found him sitting up in bed, reading one of those spy novels that had become so popular of late. He looked up at her and an expression of pure terror took over. Perhaps he couldn't see her properly. Perhaps he thought she was a ghost, or an intruder.

In point of fact, she *was* an intruder.

But she took a step forward, into the light, to reveal herself to him more fully.

"Miss Miller," he said, his gaze softening as he spoke. He placed a page-marker in his book and folded the covers shut. "I can't say I was expecting you."

"Shall I go?" Margaret asked.

He hesitated for a moment before answering, "No."

Margaret could not tell what he had on wearing from the waist down, as that portion of his body was covered by a sheet, but from the waist up he wore a simple white undershirt. His arms and shoulders were exposed. To Margaret, they looked a treat.

Her body pulsed as she beheld the man.

Setting his book on the bedside table, he asked, "Why have you come here this evening?"

Margaret found the question perplexing, as it suggested she were akin to one of his patients arriving for a doctor's visit.

She stammered, "I thought perhaps... well, you see, I thought..."

The doctor shifted his sheet, giving Margaret her first glimpse at his plain white boxer shorts. He lifted himself spryly off the mattress and circled the bed as confidently as if he had on a full suit and tie.

Placing a gentle hand on Margaret's shoulder, the doctor said, "Perhaps I was misguided in thinking—"

"No!" Margaret interrupted. "You weren't misguided, Dr. Benson! You weren't misguided at all!"

Margaret surprised herself by wrapping both arms around the nearly-naked doctor's neck and planting a forceful kiss on his mouth.

The doctor seemed genuinely shocked. He did not react to the kiss, at first, nor did he pull away or make any attempt to push Margaret aside. Perhaps he couldn't have pushed her if he'd tried, because she was holding so tightly to his neck. What mattered most to Margaret was that he made no move to press her shoulders or to pull himself from her grasp.

She went on kissing him, and eventually he returned her kiss. When he did so, the passion he brought forth was tremendous. She felt the intensity of his embrace throughout her body, and held him tighter to hers.

As they kissed, his member hardened against her thigh. She found this to be both tawdry and titillating, though what did she expect? Margaret was familiar with the male function, though this was not yet practical knowledge. What little she knew, she'd learned from books. From books, and from the inane tittle-tattle she overheard around the house. The girls with whom she lived spent quite a sum of time recounting their near-miss escapades.

Margaret had yet to see the male member in its full, fleshly glory. All she knew how to do was kiss, and so she kissed the doctor with wild abandon.

When he rode both hands under her dress, this move came as a shock. She shrieked before she could contain herself. The doctor jumped back and apologized profusely. “I'm sorry, Miss Miller. I ought never have taken the liberty.”

Margaret felt wretchedly embarrassed by her reaction. The best she could think to do was kiss him again, this time taking a daring chance by running her hands through his hair. It wasn't her intention to press him so hard against the bed, but her fortuitous force caused him to fall upon it.

She landed on top of him without breaking their kiss.

Sensing that her dress had gone askew in the back, Margaret guided the doctor's hand to her bottom. He seemed unsure, at first, but soon gave in to her insistence and exerted a gentle squeeze.

Margaret loved everything about the doctor's touch. His hands felt warm and large. Whether they were set upon her shoulder or cupping her rear, his hands aroused a swirling sensation inside of her that no other beau had evoked.

As he was spread sideways across the mattress, the doctor reached above his head to turn off the bedside lamp.

With the room cast into darkness, Margaret attempted to find the zipper that would dislodge her from her girlfriend's gown. The doctor offered a friendly chuckle as he observed her struggle, and soon asked if he could be of any assistance.

Though she was loath to break away from him, even for a brief moment, Margaret stood beside the bed and turned around. She'd forgotten the bedroom door was wide open, and quickly closed it. When she did so, the room was cast into further darkness, as most of their remaining light had been coming through the windows at the front of the house, from the streetlamps lining the doctor's residential road.

With the bedroom in near-total darkness, Margaret felt increasingly activated. As the doctor slid down her zipper, she felt as though she were a puma on the hunt, or a siren on a rock. She knew what she sought, not in her mind, but in her body. Her body held the inherited knowledge that had run through her bloodline since time immemorial: this was the will of the species.

At heart, she was animal.

At heart, so was the doctor.

LOGIC DICTATED THAT any given wedding ought to remind one of one's own, and yet Margaret never found that to be the case. Hers had been a civil affair. Ceremonies such as this—her granddaughter's wedding—struck her as excessively showy, not to mention wasteful.

Maggie and her groom were older than she and Charles had been when they'd started out on the path to marriage. Perhaps they had money to spend.

Still, what this wedding must cost!

And cost whom, she wondered. Would the bride's parents cover the expenditure?

When Margaret received her invitation, she was also invited to book a room at this luxury resort—at her own personal expense, mind. Not even a discount for the guests. She wondered if it was something of a Ponzi scheme: the hotel pays a portion of the wedding expenses in exchange for the bride and groom bringing in business.

Judging by the number of people attending Maggie and Ed's summer wedding, Windhamwood Resort was doing excellent business this weekend.

The groom awaited his bride expectantly at the end of a wooden dock. Summer sunshine glimmered across the lake. The sight could not have been more magical.

Following the flower girl's pretty procession, the bridesmaids and groomsmen went forth in the usual manner.

When Maggie's turn came to walk down the aisle, the string quartet switched its tune to the usual bridal chorus.

The man whose arm Maggie held must have been her father. Margaret could see a certain family resemblance, although she could spot more similarities between Maggie and Sharon, the mother of the bride.

And what of Sharon? Did she seem anything akin to Margaret? The woman was certainly more heavyset than Margaret had ever been, even during her pregnancy. Sharon's father had been slim, too. Hard to say where those genes came from. Even hair colour was difficult to determine, because Sharon's was clearly dyed.

Margaret longed to sense some connection between herself and her daughter, and yet all she felt was a deep and lingering estrangement. This sense certainly did not come from Sharon herself, as she had made more than one attempt to welcome Margaret into her life. Margaret knew the estrangement came from inside herself, from the emotions she'd buried long ago, which seemed too overwhelming to unearth at this point.

MANY EVENTS FROM MARGARET'S life had fallen away from memory's grasp, but there was a single moment in time she knew she would never forget.

When Margaret went to bed with Dr. Benson for the first time, she felt forever changed. She was no longer the girl she had been mere seconds earlier.

His body came as a shock to hers. In the darkness, she could not see him clearly, though he claimed he could see her silk slip glowing by the light of the moon. She felt too bashful to remove it, even when he undressed fully.

Perhaps she could see him, somewhat, though his undershirt and boxer shorts were much easier to perceive, by virtue of being immaculately white. If she tried to reflect upon the night they first made love, she could vaguely recall the shape of his shoulders, the strength in his arms. She would not allow her gaze to wander beyond his abdomen. Dark hair, there. She didn't feel it proper for a lady to look.

To this day, she could feel the press of his chest upon hers, his body sinking between her legs, his member finding the wet heat contained therein and infiltrating that uncharted area.

In that moment, the doctor was as a god to her. She would never forget how heavy his body felt upon hers, though his slim frame caused her no worry. Although her skin remained separated from his by the silk of her slip, his heat moved through her as lightning.

Did it hurt, the first time? Perhaps so. But the pain was not unwelcome, nor did she find it insufferable. It faded rather quickly, as she recalled.

He moved in her, and she moved with him. It was a wonder she knew how. She had only ever been an adequate dancer. As a general rule, her body tended not to move the way she wanted it to, and yet when she was in bed with Dr. Benson, her hips knew just what to do.

As they moved together, her hands settled upon his sides. She cautiously held to him. Thinking he must expect her to do something, though she knew not what, she dug her nails into his flesh. The act must have caused him more pain than she'd intended, because he arched away and hissed. He stayed inside her the whole while as he took hold of her hands and raised them above her head, pressing them into the pillow.

He slipped his fingers between hers.

She squeezed.

He growled, planting rapid pecks down the side of her neck. Nothing else had ever taken her breath away quite like this act. Why did it feel so good? It was only a kiss, or rather a series of kisses. Why did she feel as though her bones were turning limp and her skin set ablaze?

Margaret bent her knees, causing the doctor to arch yet higher off the bed. At first, she thought perhaps he wouldn't appreciate that she'd altered her position, but the moment that idea entered her head, Dr. Benson began thrusting so forcefully she felt him ringing through her body, from her lips down to her toes.

He picked up speed.

Her pulse quickened.

When they were bare together—or, nearly so, in Margaret's case—he brought out the beast in her.

Each thrust struck her like a blow. Her body was bliss. He released his hold on her hands and instead wrapped his arms around her waist. Gripping her tightly, he pressed his clean-shaven cheek against her chest and cried, "Miss Miller!"

"Dr. Benson," she replied, not knowing what else he might expect her to say.

His body spasmed on top of hers, causing her to cry out, though she wasn't in pain. Far from it. She felt completely enraptured by this experience they'd shared. Even if it had occurred outside the bonds of wedlock, their lovemaking felt divine.

As the doctor rested on top of her, his member pulsed wickedly within her walls. It felt larger than when they began. She wished they could stay in each other's arms for all time. In all her life, she had never felt so close to a man. She felt as though they shared a deep spiritual connection now. They were connected—physically, yes, but there was more to lovemaking than simply the act.

Now that Margaret had experienced the pleasures of the flesh, she felt queenly, otherworldly, as a goddess among women.

She was truly in the doctor's debt. They had shared something wonderful that evening. Margaret knew in her heart they would do it again and again and again.

IN ALL HER YEARS, MARGARET had never beheld a bride as keen as Maggie. The lace of her veil shimmered in the sunlight, and she appeared to shimmer as well. Sunlight illuminated her skin, though Margaret guessed the young woman would have glowed in the darkest of rooms. Her inner joy could be seen from without. She was eager to be married.

The groom, by contrast, appeared stricken by nerves. No surprises there. Charles had been the same way on their wedding day.

Margaret was not normally an emotive individual. She hadn't shed a tear at her own wedding. She'd seen no reason to. Charles had been a sensible choice, as a husband. She knew they'd get on well as a married couple, and they did. Their existence had been quiet. They'd never been consumed by the throes of passion.

At that stage in her life, Margaret had already experienced the results of passion.

That fateful summer, with Mrs. Benson and the children away at the lake house, Margaret visited the doctor almost every night under cover of darkness. The passion she felt for him could not be contained. She doubted very much she could have made it through her long days of factory work had it not been for the fantasies in which she indulged herself. Drudgery was a thing unknown to her, because her mind transported her from the factory floor to Dr. Benson's bed, which had become their nightly playground.

Later in life, Margaret became aware of the many positions lovers attempted. When she first learned of a practice involving the insertion of the male member into one's mouth, she truly could not believe this was commonly done. She felt somewhat fortunate she'd never expressed her incredulity to any living being, because apparently this has become a staple of sexual congress. Margaret had never attempted this act, nor did she wish to, but learning of its predominance in the sexual realm made her feel quite unpracticed.

Margaret was perhaps more innocent-minded than most, but she certainly was not lacking in experience. That summer with the doctor had opened her eyes to a world of pleasure she couldn't have fathomed without his assistance. The doctor's bed became more familiar to her than her own, as she slept most nights at his side—although, sleep was the last thing on her mind when she snuck through the kitchen door.

Dr. Benson was always in bed by the time Margaret ascended to the second floor. Every time she arrived at the top of the stairs, he seemed utterly shocked by her presence. The bedside light illuminated his novel. He always seemed engaged in his world of fiction. She wondered why he would not be expecting her when she came to him every night.

Once she'd entered the bedroom, she always closed the door. Her worst fear was that Mrs. Benson might come home early and find them in bed together.

The doctor greeted her by saying, “Ah! Miss Miller. How lovely to see you.”

She often felt she might persuade Dr. Benson to call her by her Christian name, but she never could work up the courage.

Of course, she never once called him Fred, and he never suggested she ought.

She could have kissed him for hours, and often they did kiss for a strikingly long while. She felt too bashful to touch him where he grew, but she did enjoy feeling his member swell against her body. Often, he would rock upon her as they kissed.

After he'd turned out the light, she felt enough at ease to remove all her clothing, including her slip and stockings. She enjoyed feeling his bare skin against hers, particularly when the night was cool. His warmth made for a welcome change.

He was not afraid to touch her—or, if he was afraid, he did it anyway. She loved to feel his hands on her chest, particularly when he thumbed her hardened buds. Oftentimes, if she found herself upon him while they necked, he would grasp her posterior with both hands and squeeze in a pulsing rhythm that seemed to match her own heartbeat.

Did their two hearts beat as one when they made love? It certainly felt that way.

Every time he entered her, she felt newly invigorated. This moment featured prominently in the fantasies that played through her mind while she packed popsicles into cardboard cartons: the ritual of reunion, their two bodies meeting at the end of each day.

When the doctor slipped his hardened member within the folds of her wet chasm, Margaret was brought to life.

As she later discovered, she was not the only one brought to life on those nights.

He moved in her. She whimpered beneath him, feeling a true sense of belonging. She parted her legs. Bending her knees, she planted her feet against the mattress. She raised her hips and lowered them as he picked up his pace.

All she could do was to follow his lead. She opened herself to him in every way she knew how. He pressed her wrists against the pillow. He kissed her neck. He grunted and moaned. He collapsed on top of her, hugging her, holding her, struggling to recover his lost breath.

She knew that he loved her. There was no need to speak the words. In fact, she'd have felt ashamed if he had spoken out loud the feelings that no doubt lived in his heart.

Despite the frequency of congress they enjoyed, Margaret never lost sight of the knowledge that Dr. Benson was wed to Mrs. Benson. They had a family together. What this meant for her, she did not know, but she was not so unworldly as to think the doctor might end his marriage so as to be with her.

Strangely, she could not imagine becoming his wife.

Every morning, Margaret awoke at five. It was not the early sun that roused her, but the doctor as he rolled out of bed.

They did not breakfast together, unless Margaret found herself desperately ravenous, and even in that case she generally ate while he was upstairs, shaving.

She quickly slipped into the dress she'd worn the night before. After sneaking out by the kitchen door, she left his property through the backyard. From the treed lot behind his house, she could exit onto the next street over, confident she had not been seen.

After a time, the girls stopped prodding her about her mystery beau. They had their own love lives with which to concern themselves. Margaret was barely a footnote, to them.

MAGGIE AND ED DIDN'T write their own vows, which was just as well. As a spectator of the wedding ceremony, Margaret enjoyed the ritual of traditional vows. Maggie smiled the whole while. She raced through the words, perhaps out of eagerness, perhaps for fear of forgetting what she ought to say next. Margaret found the show endearing.

Ed seemed nervous the whole while through. His voice cracked each time he spoke. Even from her seat in the back row, Margaret could see how firmly he grasped his bride's hands as he repeated the minister's recitation. What a lovely young man he seemed. Margaret could only hope Ed would treat her granddaughter as well as Charles had treated her throughout their many quiet years of marriage.

When the minister asked Maggie if she took this man to be her lawfully wedded husband, she bounced and squealed the words, "I do!"

When the minister asked Ed if she took this woman to be his lawfully wedded wife, he nodded solemnly. His voice broke when he said, "I do."

They were given the opportunity to kiss and took full advantage, though Ed appeared as bashful as Maggie was eager.

After they'd kissed, one of the groomsmen raced toward the couple, scooped Maggie up in his arms, and swung her toward the lake. The entire audience issued a collective gasp, and the young man set Maggie back on her feet. When she was safe again on dry land—that is to say, on the dock—the audience broke out in relieved laughter. This struck Margaret as an odd reaction. She didn't find the young man's antics at all amusing.

Perhaps the crowd was only following Maggie's lead. She had been the first to laugh.

"What a lovely ceremony," Betty said as the crowd began to rise.

"Yes, lovely," Margaret agreed.

They were informed by the minister that tea and cake would follow under the Big Top, though that's not exactly how it was phrased. All guests headed happily in that direction.

"What type of cake will it be?" Betty asked. "White, I suppose. It's generally a white cake at a wedding, though I have had a lemon cake once, and that was scrumptious. White cake isn't much to speak of, is it? I hope they chose something exciting, like a chocolate cake with fudge frosting. Wouldn't that be something else, Margaret? A chocolate cake drizzled with caramel, and with pecans scattered on top! That would be something different, wouldn't it? Margaret? Wouldn't that be something different?"

"White cake is traditional," Margaret replied distractedly. She was too busy keeping the bride and the bride's mother in her field of vision to engage properly with Betty.

"It may well be traditional, but it isn't very tasty. Now, chocolate... Margaret? Are you listening to me, Margaret? Margaret where are you going to? The tea tent is over this way. Margaret?"

Margaret hadn't realized she'd started veering toward the bride. She allowed Betty to set her on track. At any rate, it seemed as though the wedding party had pictures to take. Two photographers dressed in black were arranging the bride and groom, along with their respective families and friends, by the lakeside, where the afternoon sun sparkled boldly off the still water.

If life had turned her in a different direction, Margaret herself would be lining up for that photograph. Perhaps she and Maggie would share their own little vignette. And then another photo with Maggie, her mother, and Margaret: three generations of women brought together in celebration.

WHEN SHE REFLECTED on that time in her life, Margaret found it practically absurd that neither she nor the doctor had taken precautions to prevent pregnancy. It's not as though she were unaware of such matters. And the doctor would have been even more versant in both current and traditional techniques.

Perhaps the doctor wished for more children, but Mrs. Benson did not.

Perhaps he had purposefully impregnated Margaret.

Ah, but all was speculation. Dr. Benson had long since died, and Mrs. Benson was gone, too. One could only guess at their intentions.

By the time Margaret found herself in the family way, autumn was calling and classes had resumed. Initially, she attributed the nausea she experienced each morning to anxiousness about returning to school. Her courses were notoriously challenging, and she couldn't be sure she was up to the task.

When it finally occurred to Margaret that she might be pregnant, she went to Dr. Benson. By that point in the year, Mrs.

Benson and the children had arrived home from the lake house, but Margaret felt no apprehension in visiting the doctor. At the heart of the matter, she'd only gone to consult him on a medical matter.

They had quite reasonably decided to put an end to their nightly ritual of making love in his bed as soon as his wife's return grew imminent. Perhaps, if she were honest, she would admit that she missed the doctor quite a lot. She missed his body most especially when she was alone at night. She missed feeling his skin on hers. She missed his kisses and his hands. She missed telling him all the factory gossip.

Margaret's stomach tossed like a boat on an angry sea as she knocked at the doctor's door.

Mrs. Benson answered wearing a striking blue dress that fitted snugly. Her hair was done up elegantly. She had on a stunning set of diamond earrings set in silver or white gold, or possibly platinum. She looked as though she were ready for a night on the town, which inspired Margaret to say, "I hope I'm not interrupting anything, Mrs. Benson. It looks as though you're going out, perhaps. I can come back at a later date, if it's more convenient."

The doctor's wife gave Margaret a perplexed look. "No, in fact I've only just arrived home." Recognition sparked and she said, "Trixie, isn't it? Do come in. The children will be so glad to see you."

"That's nice of you to say, Mrs. Benson, only it's Margaret—not Trixie."

"Margaret. Yes, Margaret. Of course. The children are playing out back. Would you like to join them, or I shall call them in?"

As Mrs. Benson shuffled her into the house, Margaret said, "In point of fact, I've come for Dr. Benson."

Mrs. Benson's eyes flashed.

"There's a medical matter I wish to discuss with him."

"Oh, I see." In a conspiratorial hush, Mrs. Benson said, "In that case, I won't inform the children you've arrived. My husband is in his office." Mrs. Benson led the way, knocking gently when she arrived at the doctor's door. "Fred," she said as she opened it a crack. "There's a young lady here to see you."

The doctor appeared nonplussed, though only momentarily. A quick smile drew across his lips as he said, "Miss Miller! To what do I owe the pleasure?"

Softly, as though she could smell the pregnancy on Margaret's skin, Mrs. Benson said, "I shall leave you to it. Can I get you a cup of tea, young Margie?"

"No, thank you," Margaret replied.

"The kettle is just boiled. I can have a pot brewed in two shakes. Just let me know, all right?"

Margaret nodded solemnly. The woman's graciousness tore at Margaret's heartstrings, and she wondered how she would get through this conversation without flooding the doctor's office in tears.

Once Mrs. Benson had gone and closed the door, the doctor's expression fell. "Please, Miss Miller, do have a seat."

Margaret sat at the edge of the chair opposite the doctor's desk, unable to meet his gaze.

He made no reference to their former relationship, and instead treated her as she imagined he would any patient. "What can I help you with today?"

She blurted out the words, "I think I'm pregnant."

When she glanced up at his face, she noted very little reaction. Much less of a reaction than she had anticipated, considering he would be the baby's father—if there was a baby to speak of.

He asked her a series of questions, though he already knew the answers to many. When he asked about various symptoms, there were a good number she hadn't yet experienced, or at least hadn't taken note of.

"Now that classes have started up again, my mind has been occupied by my schooling," she explained. "Perhaps, if I'd been paying more attention to my physical health, I would have noted such occurrences."

The doctor assured her that every pregnancy is different, and most women experience a selection of symptoms—not all of the above. At any rate, they hadn't conducted the test yet.

"What is involved?" Margaret asked, suspecting she knew the answer, but not willing to make any outward statements.

Dr. Benson explained that a urine sample must be collected, which would be analyzed in a laboratory. The answer as to whether or not Margaret were pregnant would be forthcoming in two weeks' time.

"Two weeks?" Margaret choked. "Could you perhaps find out sooner than that? Two weeks is a dreadfully long time to wait when one wonders what life holds in store."

The doctor chuckled paternally, as though he were playing the role of her father on a television comedy. He told her he would see what he could do, and then handed her a glass beaker and told her she was welcome to use the restroom upstairs.

Mrs. Benson intercepted her as she left the doctor's office, beaker in hand. "The test is nothing to be afraid of, Margie. Can I call you Margie?"

"I'd rather—"

"I can sit with you, if you'd like."

More brusquely than was her intention, Margaret said, "Thank you, but I know how to use the toilet."

Mrs. Benson appeared hurt, but she recovered in time to usher Margaret upstairs. "I still remember my first test. Oh, my heart was in my belly the whole while!" Leaning close, the lady of the house confessed, "When I found out the deal was done, I can't tell you how I was enthralled. Prior to that, I'd hinted to Fred that I wished to be wed, but a serious medical man like him would never have married a silly ol' flirt like yours truly—not without a large dose of persuasion."

Margaret was so taken aback by Mrs. Benson's revelation that she didn't notice they were standing in the bathroom together. When Mrs. Benson closed the door, Margaret asked, "Do you mean to say your eldest was born out of wedlock?"

"Goodness, no!" Mrs. Benson giggled. "Not *born* out of wedlock, heavens, no! But conceived? Well, that's another matter entirely." She shrugged and looked over her shoulder. "If you're itching for a hitching, there's no better way to convince a lad the time is nigh. I don't see any ring on your finger, Miss Margie, but I'd bet it won't stay bare for long. You tell your young man what's what, and he's sure to come around."

"I have my doubts."

In her mind, Margaret pictured some imaginary young man—no person she had ever met, nor even a cinema star—who could fill in as her baby's father for the purpose of this conversation. Margaret could hardly confess that the only man with whom she had ever been intimate was this woman's own husband.

"You mark my word," Mrs. Benson said, wagging her finger conspiratorially. "Tell your young man he must marry you or you will be his ruin. If he won't listen to reason, go to his parents. They'll talk some sense into him."

Margaret grimaced. "If only that were possible."

"Does your young man have no parents?" Mrs. Benson asked. "Is he an orphan like yourself?"

Where on earth did Mrs. Benson get the idea that Margaret was an orphan? The suggestion nearly brought laughter to her lips, but she was able to stifle it long enough to press the lady of the house from the room.

"If you'll excuse me, I could use a moment of privacy," Margaret said as she closed the door and secured the lock.

She looked at the beaker in her hand before turning her gaze to the door. When she considered how kind the lady of the house had been after Margaret spent the summer in bed with her husband, an ache erupted in her chest. This was a pain beyond tears.

When she emerged from the bathroom with a warm beaker of urine in hand, Mrs. Benson stood in the hallway waiting for her. "You'll be beside yourself for the next two weeks as you await the news."

"I sincerely think not," Margaret replied. "The test is a formality. I already know I'm pregnant.

WITH BETTY AT HER SIDE, Margaret wandered toward the tent where tea and finger sandwiches were being served alongside a spread of dainty desserts.

"Look at all these goodies!" Betty cried, forcing her way past the lineup.

Margaret felt absolutely humiliated by Betty's behaviour, and apologized to everyone she snuck by. At this point in every excursion, Margaret wondered why on earth she chose to go anywhere with batty old Betty. The easy answer was that Margaret, herself, was a batty old woman and their polar personalities complemented one another.

Without Betty to force her way through the crowd, Margaret would have waited patiently and respectfully in the lineup of wedding guests. Eventually, her feet would have ached badly enough that she'd be forced to sit down and she would never get to eat any of the sandwiches and treats Betty served them.

"They put out these tiny plates," Betty explained, "so people won't take too much. The only thing to do is pile up your food. It's that or take two plates. There's no coming back for seconds. By the time you come back, all the good stuff will be gone."

Margaret gazed longingly at the large urns of coffee and tea. If she drank too much of either, she would spend the whole drive home desperate for a bathroom.

That is to say, if she went home in Betty's car. Perhaps the day would not end that way. Perhaps Margaret would get up the courage to introduce herself to the woman who'd invited her here: to her daughter, Sharon.

Maggie would set off on her honeymoon, of course. A young woman couldn't be expected to put wedding plans aside in order to entertain the grandmother she never knew. After wishing the bride a warm goodbye, Sharon would surely sit down with Margaret and catch her up on all the years they'd missed. They might end up gabbing into the night, and Sharon would say it was too late to leave; they ought to stay the night at this lovely resort.

When Betty arrived at the multi-tiered wedding cake, she glanced around in confusion. "Where's the knife? How are we supposed to serve ourselves if they don't put out a knife?"

"Don't you dare lay a finger on that cake!" Margaret snapped. "The first cut must be made by the bride and groom. Have you never been to a wedding?"

Betty pouted. "Well, when do you suppose they're going to cut into it?"

Margaret turned in the direction of the wedding party, but she couldn't see past the hoards of guests. Glancing that way gave her a sense of claustrophobia, and she returned her gaze to Betty before saying, "The bride and groom are currently occupied."

Betty's brow went up. "I dare say!"

"With the wedding photos!" Margaret declared, feeling increasingly irritated with every passing moment. "Once the photos are taken, they will surely cut the cake."

Betty gazed at the tiered structure forlornly.

"Not five minutes ago you were complaining that you're never impressed by the taste of a wedding cake. And look at all you've got on your plate! Those gateaux would last any normal person a month of Sundays, so quit your complaining and let's get ourselves a cuppa."

"Very well," Betty said, sullenly, as Margaret marched her toward the urns.

WHEN THE TEST RESULTS came in, Dr. Benson summoned Margaret to his house. Mrs. Benson was not at home when she arrived, and neither were the children.

The doctor greeted Margaret at the door with an amiable smile. He invited her inside without seeming afraid of what the neighbours might think. After escorting her into his office, he closed the door even though they were alone in the house. Once he'd seated himself in the chair across from hers, he gave her the news.

Margaret was not floored by the results of her pregnancy test. Her body had made it increasingly obvious, over the two weeks prior, that she was indeed carrying the doctor's child. She did, however, feel heat rising through her body, up her neck and into her cheeks, when Dr. Benson said, "Let's discuss what happens next."

Her heart fluttered. She didn't notice, until moments later, that she had placed both hands protectively upon her belly.

"I've discussed the matter with Norma," the doctor went on. "My wife has agreed that the best thing for it would be if you came to live with us. We are well equipped to take care of you, here. You, in turn, could chip in around the household, helping Norma with childcare and meal preparation if you wish."

"Of course I would help out," Margaret replied, though she hadn't fully considered what the doctor was suggesting. "Would Mrs. Benson truly wish for me to live here with you? In your family home?"

"Indeed she would," the doctor said. "It was her idea for you to come here. Her heart went out to you, after seeing you the other week. She said you remind her of herself at that age."

Margaret's stomach turned. She couldn't be sure whether the pregnancy was to blame, or if it was the thought of living under the same roof as the wife of the man who'd put her in the family way.

"You would make a welcome addition to our bustling household," the doctor went on. "We would be only to pleased to take you in."

"But what about..." Margaret trailed off, not knowing how to ask such a delicate question. "Will Mrs. Benson not feel... oh, how shall I put it? Will she not be upset when she discovers who fathered my child?"

Dr. Benson wore his familiar fatherly smile when he said, "Norma has been made aware of the situation surrounding your delicate condition."

Margaret's stomach clenched. "You told her about... our *liaison*?"

Evading Margaret's gaze, the doctor said, "There will be no need to discuss the matter further. Doing so would only be hurtful to Norma, especially when she's shown you such a high degree of compassion."

"Of course," Margaret replied. "I understand completely. Only, I can't help wondering, Doctor: wasn't your wife upset when she learned the news? Didn't she pop a gasket? If any husband of mine—"

"Miss Miller," the doctor growled, cutting her off abruptly. "We will speak no more of this." He took a long breath while gazing down at some papers on his desk. When he spoke again, he sounded considerably calmer. "My wife has extended a very generous offer. She is willing to take you in when, I gather from all you've told me, your own mother would likely throw you to the dogs. In your condition, you have few options. I believe Norma's plan to be the best for your health and well-being."

"I agree," Margaret said eagerly. She did not wish to lose out on the opportunity to join the doctor's household. "But, Dr. Benson, don't you fear that it will put undue pressure on us both, to be living under the same roof? Considering our history and all?"

"We must put the past behind us," the doctor said, tugging self-assuredly at his waistcoat. "I grant you, it won't be easy, considering the... chemistry..."

Margaret blushed and the doctor cleared his throat.

"But we are adults," he went on. "We are perfectly capable of controlling our impulses if we wish to do so. And if you are to live under this roof, do so we must."

"Agreed," Margaret said.

"Very good." He stood and offered a hand to shake. "Then we have a plan. How long will it take you to pack your things? Norma has offered her assistance, and I would be happy to lend the Merc."

Margaret felt quite startled. "You'd like for me to move in right away? But what about school?"

"I should think you'd give up your place this year."

Margaret's heart slumped. She tried to draw on the dregs of her draining ambition, but she knew the doctor was right. Already, she felt herself unable to focus in class and while studying.

If she were no longer a student, there would be no place for her in student accommodations.

How fortunate that Mrs. Benson had taken kindly to her, despite her indiscretions. If Margaret had a husband and he took up with another woman, Margaret would surely throw a fit, not extend that woman a warm invitation to stay with the family.

The situation in which she found herself sounded like a fairy story. She felt she ought to pinch herself.

Surely this was a dream.

AS THE HAPPY COUPLE prepared to cut the cake, Sharon took out her cell phone and started snapping photos.

"Mother!" the bride said, with a lighthearted grin. "You don't need to take pictures. That's why we hired photographers."

"At considerable personal expense," added the man at Sharon's side—her husband, presumably. He seemed an amiable sort, and the pair looked happy together . What more could Margaret want for her only daughter?

The photographers did indeed take pictures while Maggie and Ed cut the cake, but Sharon continued to do so as well. She wanted to have these pictures on her phone, she told her husband.

Sharon knew her own mind, which was a quality Margaret valued in women. Her adoptive parents had clearly raised her to be a cheerful and strong human being. They'd done a fine job, as Margaret knew they would. She'd never have left her child with anyone who wasn't up to the task.

Though she sometimes questioned the doctor's motives these many decades later, at the time she thought him pure as gold.

Mrs. Benson doted on Margaret throughout her gestative months, to the extent that the lady of the house would sit on the tub ledge and stroke her back while Margaret leaned over the toilet bowl feeling certain she was about to lose her breakfast.

Though Mrs. Benson often encouraged Margaret to call her Norma, Margaret was unable to do so.

They never once discussed the affair that had landed Margaret in her current predicament.

Margaret found the quality of mercy the doctor's wife showed her worthy of beatification. Who would have anticipated a flighty and seemingly simple-headed woman like Mrs. Benson to be capable of such saintly levels of forgiveness?

At first, Margaret wondered if perhaps Mrs. Benson didn't love her husband. Had she perhaps only married him in hopes of attaining wealth and stature?

After only a few days of living alongside the family, she knew this was far from true. Mrs. Benson mooned over the doctor, casting doe-eyed glances in his direction when she thought he wasn't looking. Margaret wasn't sure whether the doctor took note of his wife's loving gaze, but Margaret herself couldn't help but see what was before her: Mrs. Benson adored her husband, and he loved her every bit as much as he adored their darling children.

Oftentimes, Margaret questioned her own lack of jealousy. As the doctor's former lover, ought she not feel hard done by? When the doctor complimented his wife on the chic new frock she'd bought herself in town, why did Margaret not wish the doctor were complimenting her?

True, she looked dowdy in Mrs. Benson's old maternity clothes, but a loyal lover only ever saw beauty before him.

There's no telling why Margaret lacked envy when she watched the doctor and his wife cuddle up by the fire: the doctor reading his newspaper while Mrs. Benson sat on the arm of his chair, rustling his dark brown locks in a most loving manner.

The doctor and Mrs. Benson made for a most attractive couple.

Margaret, for her part, looked gawkish at the doctor's side. Mrs. Benson must have wondered what he ever saw in her. Perhaps she did not fear that Margaret would steal her husband away from her because she was ever so confident in her own attractiveness.

Although, from what Margaret had observed of beautiful women, a great many of them are sorely lacking in self-esteem.

Clearly, this was not the case with Mrs. Benson.

In the delivery room, Mrs. Benson stayed with Margaret. Margaret was glad to have her there. At the hospital, her surroundings felt both stark and hectic. She was only too pleased to have a familiar face to look at. Also, Mrs. Benson had given birth to three babies, and had innumerable words of guidance.

When Sharon was born at last, Margaret felt as though she were living in a dream. Her child did not seem real. Margaret felt as though an angel had come to pay her a visit. She feared the feeling could not last.

Yet, the feeling has lasted throughout these many years, these decades. The feeling of being visited by an angelic little bundle resided within Margaret even when Dr. Benson secured her a placement in a nursing school quite a distance away from the doctor's home and practice. The feeling remained even when he assured her it would be for the best if he and his wife adopted baby Sharon. That way, Margaret could continue her education, earn her nursing credentials, and perhaps one day enjoy a normal life with a husband of her own.

"There's no need for you to be weighed down by one experience," the doctor remarked.

Margaret found his phrasing odd. How could she feel weighed down by her child? Nothing else in life had so uplifted her.

But Dr. Benson had a way of explaining matters that made Margaret feel as though he knew what was best not only for her, but for her baby as well. After spending so many months in the doctor's home, she knew it to be a loving and supportive environment. Margaret had judged Mrs. Benson too harshly upon meeting the woman. This was possibly due to Mrs. Benson's refined looks and fine dress. One often assumes women like Mrs. Benson are no good with children, but the lady of the house had proved that to be untrue. She doted on her little ones as much as she'd doted on Margaret throughout her months of pregnancy, as well as during her recovery period following the birth.

Margaret had no doubt the doctor and Mrs. Benson would provide Sharon with not only the necessities of life, but the joys of family.

The doctor was not remiss in reminding Margaret that she would experience considerable difficulty in finding a husband if she went about the world with a baby on her hip. Without a husband, she would need to find herself a job. And yet how could she work when there was a baby to care for? If she could not work, she would have no money. She would have no support.

No, that wouldn't do for the child.

Margaret's baby deserved everything life had to offer. The doctor and Mrs. Benson could provide for Sharon. Difficult as it would be to leave her little bundle and take off for nursing school, Dr. Benson assured Margaret this would be best. She had no reason to believe he might be mistaken. She did what she believed would be best for her child, regardless of her innermost feelings.

A mother must make sacrifices, and this was hers. She allowed the doctor and his wife to adopt Sharon because she loved her so, because she cared more about her baby's future than her own emotions.

Many tears would fall, but Margaret did not question her decision.

ONCE THE CAKE WAS CUT, servers made their way to each table, offering small plates with small pieces to each guest.

"Why is this taking so long?" Betty harrumphed. "Goodness, if we sit here waiting we'll never get a slice. I'm going up there to cut one myself."

Normally, Margaret would have told her friend to quiet down and wait her turn, but on this occasion, Betty's departure was to her benefit.

As soon as Betty shuffled toward the wedding cake, Margaret carved a stealthy path toward the table where Sharon sat. She did not take the most direct route. Betty would surely see her if she did. Instead, she meandered toward the edge of the tent. Many guests had taken their cake slices out into the sun, where adults chatted, where small children danced

A server carrying four cake plates stopped Margaret to ask, "Is everything all right, ma'am? Can I help you find what you're looking for?"

Margaret grunted nastily. She offered no reply as she made her way around the young person. Now that she felt driven to action, she wouldn't let anyone stand in her way.

"Oh, you didn't know?" said someone in the crowd.

Everyone was chatting about something or other, but this woman's tone caught Margaret's ear particularly. She sounded as though she were about to spill a lifetime's worth of gossip.

The woman lowered her voice and whispered, "Sharon only told me about it quite recently. Fred and Norma weren't really her parents—her biological parents, I should say. Turns out she was adopted."

"No," replied the person with whom the gossip spoke. "Does Sharon know her real parents? Does she know who they are?"

Margaret's skin went cold, though she felt as if she were burning up inside. The rest of the chatter fell away. All she could hear were these two voices in the crowd. Beyond the gossips, she could have heard a pin drop. Her ears filled with a piercing, oddly amplified sort of silence.

"I don't think Sharon's met her real mother—*birth mother* is what Sharon calls her. I couldn't tell you the woman's name."

"Why did she give up her baby? Does Sharon know?"

"Yes, her father told her—that is to say Fred told her—before he died."

"And?"

And?

And?

"And apparently her birth mother was basically a child, herself, when she got pregnant. Fifteen years old, from what Sharon tells me."

The fellow gossip clucked her teeth. "Fifteen! So young!"

Fifteen? In no world was Margaret fifteen when she got pregnant. She was twenty-one if she was a day! Why did Sharon think her birth mother had been a teenager? Who might have told her such drivel?

"And the father?" the fellow gossip asked. "Who was the father in all this?"

"No one knows. Apparently Sharon's poor mother was taken against her will by a young man in her acquaintance."

"A likely story!"

"Karen! Don't be uncharitable."

"I'm only saying it's easy enough for a young lady to make such a claim when she finds herself in trouble. That's the problem with young people: they don't take responsibility for their actions. The moment they find themselves in hot water, they blame someone else for their mistakes."

Karen went on and on, but Margaret, in her utter confusion, blocked out the woman's truly unpleasant voice.

Why did that woman, whoever she was, believe Sharon's father to be a neighbourhood tough or some such individual? Why did she think Margaret had been coerced? At fifteen? This was far from the truth.

The gossipmonger said herself she was informed—that is to say, misinformed—of these matters by Sharon. Which meant Sharon believed these false rumours to be true.

Sharon knew that the woman who raised her was not her biological mother. And yet it would seem Dr. Benson neglected to mention that he was, in point of fact, her father in every sense of the word.

From what Margaret could now piece together, it would seem that Sharon knew Margaret to be her mother, but Sharon figured her father was some unknown man.

That meant the letter Sharon had written to Margaret, the one Margaret found so deeply forgiving, had been based on an acceptance of falsehoods, not facts. Sharon had no idea her father had cheated on her mother with Margaret.

Perhaps Norma never knew, either.

It never occurred to Margaret until that moment, but perhaps Dr. Benson had fabricated this story of Margaret having been the subject of coercion when he discussed her situation with his wife. Perhaps Mrs. Benson never knew she was raising her husband's daughter—a daughter planted, by adulterous means, in another woman's womb.

Margaret felt faint when she reflected on this possibility. She looked around for an unoccupied chair and spotted a few, but they were all tucked at tables occupied by other guests. She would rather stand on unsteady legs than sit at a table with strangers and be forced to explain why she had suddenly collapsed in their midst.

The same young server who had shown concern for Margaret earlier, and whom she had so rudely pushed past, approached her again. This time, when he asked her if she was feeling all right, she shook her head to indicate no.

"Let's get you some fresh air," he said, leading her from the tent and parking her in a chair that was shaded from the sun. He sat alongside her, but not before fetching her a bottle of water. "The heat gets to people," he said. "We've gotta take care of each other."

Margaret told the young man it wasn't the heat, but emotion, getting the best of her. She rambled at length. Though she didn't intend to, she spilled the contents of her heart and mind to this stranger.

"My daughter believes I was fifteen when I became pregnant, but that isn't true. I was twenty-one. She was told her father was a boy from the neighbourhood who had taken me against my will, but this is also a lie. Dr. Benson is her father and always will be."

The young man nodded gently, though his eyes expressed confusion. She realized she was gripping his hand, but she didn't let go.

"She wrote me the most wonderful letter," Margaret went on, now intent on proving to the server she was indeed in full possession of her mental faculties. "I should say, my daughter wrote to me. Sharon. She's the mother of the bride, which makes me the bride's grandmother. Only, Maggie and I have never met. I was unmarried, and I gave up my baby to a couple who could raise her well. I realize now that she was misinformed about my situation, you see. She wrote me the loveliest letter inviting me into her life, but her understanding is based on an acceptance of falsehoods."

"Have another sip of water," the server said. "Your face is getting really red."

Margaret tightened her grip on the young man's hand. "Her father and I enjoyed a love affair. I've never said those words out loud. I've never admitted this to anyone. You're the first."

"I'm flattered," replied the young man, though he winced when she dug her nails into his skin.

"How would my daughter feel about me if she were to find out the truth? Her father cheated on her mother—with me—and she was conceived as a result. Not only would she lose respect for me, but she would likely lose respect for her father as well."

"You don't know that," the young man said as he attempted to twist his hand out of her grip. "And even if she does lose a bit of respect for you, or for him, or both, she'll get over it after a while. It's better for people to know the truth."

Margaret loosened her hold on the young man, and he sighed. So did she. He encouraged her to drink some water, and at last she did.

She took a moment to consider the young man's words, but how could she take advice from someone who lacked her degree of life experience?

"Do you have children?" she asked the young man.

"No, but—"

"I simply can't imagine telling my daughter the truth when it's sure to cause her harm."

The server said, "The truth might sting a bit, but I doubt it'll harm her."

Perhaps he was right. "She invited me into her life based on a lie she was told."

"She invited you into her life because she wants you in her life," the boy reasoned. "If she didn't want you in her life, she wouldn't have invited you."

Margaret could feel her resistance crumbling. "I came here today with every intention of introducing myself to my daughter for the first time. Now that I'm here, I'm beginning to realize I'm not up to the task. I'm looking for any excuse to hide away."

The server nodded knowingly. "I can come with you, if you want. Just for moral support. If that helps."

He winced and she realized she'd once again dug her fingernails into the soft skin of his hand. She consciously released her hold on the young man once she came to understand he had no intention of running.

WHEN SHE WAS AWAY AT nursing school, Margaret wrote letters to Dr. and Mrs. Benson each week. She asked after Sharon, of course, and inquired as to the other children. She informed the doctor of what she was learning in her courses, and thanked him on an ongoing basis for securing her a spot at such a prestigious school. She could never have gotten in on her own, and she'd never have had the money to pay without his assistance.

She really did consider him to be her hero, in those days.

And if the doctor was a hero, she considered Mrs. Benson no less than a heroine. Not only was the woman caring for Margaret's baby while raising three other children, but also taking the time to send photographs and care packages in the mail. Margaret appreciated the trinkets and baked goods, of course, but she treasured the pictures of Sharon above all her worldly possessions.

Mrs. Benson signed her letters "Norma," and yet Margaret never could work up the nerve to address her as such. She had far too much respect for the woman who had adopted her baby.

As the pressures of practical training began, Margaret struggled to make time for letter-writing. Mrs. Benson's lengthy missives grew shorter and less frequent. Margaret apologized for her scant communications, thinking she had put off the woman who was caring for her child. When she received no reply, she placed a long-distance telephone call to the doctor's home. Mrs. Benson answered, but her voice sounded different, somehow. She seemed distracted, although with four young children to care for, this should come as no surprise.

Even so, Margaret felt odd after her brief conversation with the lady of the house, and thought about it often throughout the week.

When she telephoned again, her call went unanswered.

At the end of term, Margaret planned to stay with her parents over the holidays, but they responded, coolly, that she needn't bother troubling herself. Just as well, because she would rather spend Christmas with the doctor's family. She missed the scent of her daughter's head and longed to cradle that bundle in her arms.

She set down her suitcase at the base of the front steps and fizzed with anticipation as she knocked at the door.

The woman who answered was not familiar to Margaret. Perhaps the doctor and Mrs. Benson had taken on a housekeeper or a nanny.

"Hello," Margaret said. "Are Dr. and Mrs. Benson at home?"

The strange woman cocked her head, looking puzzled. She informed Margaret that the doctor and his family had moved away. Margaret stared, awestruck. They couldn't have moved away. Why would they? The doctor's practice was here in town. Where would they have moved to? And why?

She felt sure the family must be in the house, and fought the urge to push past the woman, in search of familiar faces. Instead, she asked, "Did the doctor leave a forwarding address?"

"I'm afraid not," the woman told her before closing the door in her face.

Margaret didn't know what to do. She stood outside the house until she noticed the woman peeking through the curtains. She then carried her suitcase to the sidewalk, looking up and down the street as though she had stepped into another world.

She knocked at a number of doors, asking the neighbours if they knew where the doctor had moved to, but nobody had a clue, and if they did, they regarded her with so much suspicion it was doubtful they would tell her, anyway.

All she could think to do was drag her luggage to the house in which she'd once lived. There were still a few girls of her acquaintance living there. Margaret allowed them to drag her to a Christmas party, where she drank a considerable amount of alcohol. She spent the next three days on the bathroom floor, but she didn't learn any lessons from the experience.

She allowed the girls to drag her out at New Year's Eve, as well.

Once she'd returned to nursing school, Margaret reviewed the letters Mrs. Benson had written her. In all her communications, the woman never once referred to Baby Sharon as "your daughter" or any such phrasing as that. The notes were cheerful and involved, but they read as those that would be sent to a family friend and not the mother of one's adoptive child.

Margaret was never quite sure how she got through that year. She must have thrown herself into her studies and practical skills development, concentrating all her energy away from her heartbreak. That pain resided so deeply inside her that she had to close the door to it in order to survive.

In time, she found employment in her chosen field. She met Charles after a girl at work went on one date with him, characterized him as a "perfect bore," and passed him off onto Margaret. He was indeed a perfect bore—perhaps even *the* perfect bore—and they married after a respectable courtship period.

Margaret and Charles enjoyed a satisfactory life together until he left this earth, dying suddenly in his sleep.

In all their years of marriage, she never told him about the child she'd borne before they met. She closed off the portion of her heart that held her baby tight. She acted as if that fragment of her life were some fiction she'd invented to wile away the hours.

She went on with life, feeling always somewhat guilty, always somewhat alone.

And now she had the opportunity to amend her missteps. Her daughter had sent her this invitation. Sharon wanted Margaret in her life, bless her. And Margaret had come all this way to answer the call.

Rising from her seat, Margaret said to the young server, "I think I might be ready."

"I think you definitely are," he replied.

She held the young man's hand, but did not move. What if she told Sharon the truth about her relationship with the doctor, and Sharon rejected her? She would not only ruin her chance to repair her relationship with her daughter, but she would ruin her granddaughter's wedding day as well.

Margaret smiled faintly at the young man by her side, but her thoughts drifted toward deception: what if she never told Sharon the actual truth? What if she went along with the less hurtful version of events, the one Sharon already believed to be true? Then she could build a relationship with her daughter, albeit one based on a lie.

Her heart trilled. Whether she told Sharon the truth or went along with the fiction Dr. Benson had created, this was not a decision she needed to make in the moment. She hadn't yet introduced herself to her daughter. One thing at a time.

The young server accompanied Margaret into the dining tent. She leaned on him for support.

"Everything okay?" another server asked him.

He nodded and said, "Just fine. Something I need to take care of, then I'll get back to work."

"I'm sorry," Margaret said to him. "I've taken up too much of your time already. I should let you go."

"No way," he said, clasping a warm arm around her. "I told you I'd come with you, and I'm not going back on my word. We're in this together."

She cherished his warmth and selflessness, focusing on her intense gratitude rather than the anxiety creeping through her system as she approached the table where her daughter sat.

"There she is," Margaret whispered to the server. "That's my Sharon."

He gripped her arm tighter, lending support.

Sharon's husband seemed to be off somewhere. His seat was vacated, at any rate. Margaret made her way toward it as Sharon gazed lovingly at the beautiful bride, Margaret's granddaughter.

What a perfect day. Why would Margaret risk ruining it?

The server at her side must have sensed her apprehension, because he urged her onward before she could turn tail and run.

When they reached their destination, Sharon glanced up at them, first looking at the server and then at Margaret. The moment their gazes locked, Margaret felt a fear the likes of which she'd never experienced. But that fear faded into hope as she watched her daughter's expression turn quizzical, and then alter to one of intense recognition.

Sharon leapt from her chair. With an optimistic lilt in her voice, she asked, "Have we... do we... know each other?"

Margaret wasn't sure how to answer. She felt as though she were taking ages to speak when finally she responded, "Not yet. But we will." Extending her hand, she said, "I'm Margaret."

The young server released Margaret's arm just in time for Sharon to wrap her in the hug of a lifetime. Margaret felt stunned, unsure how to react. She wondered if people were watching, and what they might say.

Such thoughts melted away when her daughter gripped her tightly. "I'm so glad you decided to come. I've wanted to meet you for so long, and now you're finally here!"

"At last," Margaret agreed, wrapping her daughter in her arms. "At long last."

Other Titles in Giselle Renarde's Wedding Heat series include:

Season One:
One in the Hand
Two in the Bush
Skinny Dipping
Pretty Bride3
MILF of the Groom
If the Shoes Fit
Season Two:
Hole in One
Full Service Bridesmaid
Swing Low
Catering to the Masses
Lickity Split
Wife Watching
Season Three:
Saturday Night Sex Show
Bachelor Party
Happy Ever After

ABOUT GISELLE RENARDE

Giselle Renarde is an award-winning queer Canadian writer. Nominated Toronto's Best Author in NOW Magazine's 2015 Readers' Choice Awards, her fiction has appeared in well over 100 short story anthologies, including prestigious collections like Best Lesbian Romance, Best Women's Erotica, and the Lambda Award-winning collection Take Me There, edited by Tristan Taormino. Giselle's juicy novels include Anonymous, Cherry, Nanny State, Ondine, Seven Kisses, The Other Side of Ruth, and the Lesbian Diaries series.

Giselle Renarde

Canada just got hotter!

Want to stay up to date? Visit

http://donutsdesires.blogspot.com[1]

Sign up for Giselle's newsletter: http://eepurl.com/R4b11

1. http://donutsdesires.blogspot.com/

www.ingramcontent.com/pod-product-compliance
Ingram Content Group UK Ltd.
Pitfield, Milton Keynes, MK11 3LW, UK
UKHW021934190726
13853UKWH00004B/1445

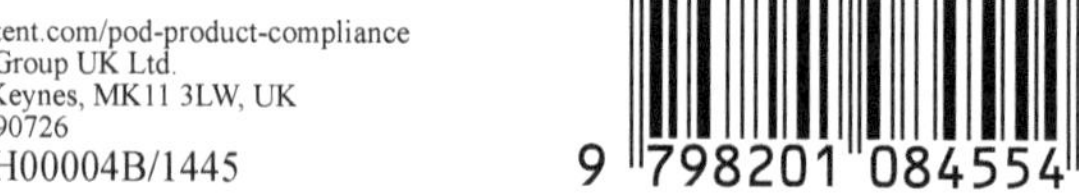